THE TIMELY ADVENTURES of
CAPTAIN CLOCK

Franklin Watts
First published in Great Britain in 2018
by The Watts Publishing Group

1 3 5 7 9 10 8 6 4 2

Credits
Art: Pol Cunyat
Design Manager: Peter Scoulding
Cover Designer: Cathryn Gilbert
Production Manager: Robert Dale
Series Consultant: Paul Register
Executive Editor: Adrian Cole

HB ISBN 978 1 4451 5714 6
PB ISBN 978 1 4451 5715 3
Library ebook ISBN 978 1 4451 5716 0

Printed in China

MIX
Paper from
responsible sources
FSC
www.fsc.org   FSC® C104740

Franklin Watts
An imprint of
Hachette Children's Group
Part of The Watts Publishing Group
Carmelite House
50 Victoria Embankment
London EC4Y 0DZ

An Hachette UK Company
www.hachette.co.uk

www.franklinwatts.co.uk

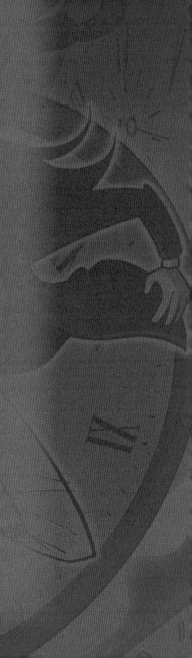

THE TIMELY ADVENTURES of
CAPTAIN CLOCK

TONY LEE AND POL CUNYAT

LONDON·SYDNEY

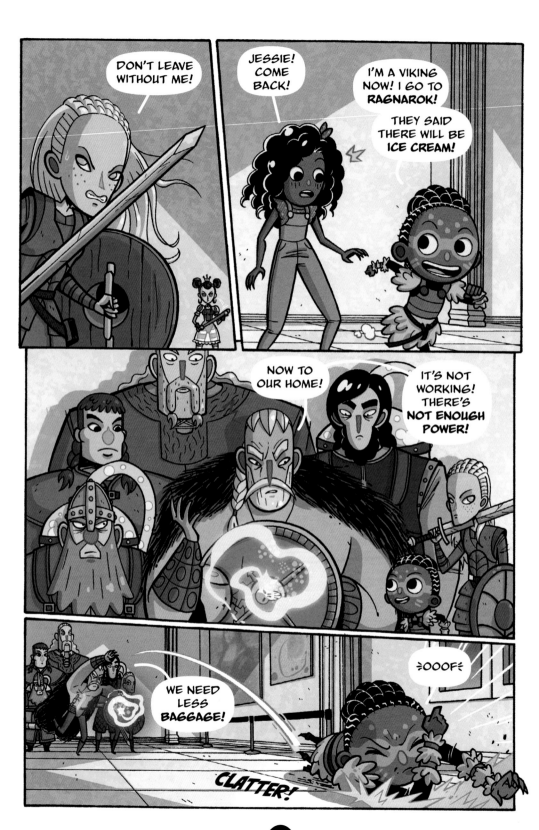

LONDON - PRESENT DAY.

HERE YOU GO, GIRLS! THE **EXACT TIME AND PLACE** YOU LEFT!

THANKS, CAPTAIN CLOCK! GOOD LUCK FINDING THE TIME VIKINGS!

HOLD ON - THIS ISN'T RIGHT.

WHY ARE THE PEOPLE DRESSED LIKE **VIKINGS** --

-- AND WHEN DID **THAT** GET HERE?

HELLO, WE'RE DOING A **SCHOOL PROJECT.**

WHEN DID THE VIKINGS WIN?

YOU MEAN WHEN DID **KING YORGEN THE FIRST** RULE?

THAT WAS AFTER HE BEAT **ALFRED THE PRETENDER** IN **878 CE.**

878 IS WHEN ALFRED 'THE GREAT' **DEFEATED** THE VIKINGS AND MADE PEACE WITH THEM.

HE WASN'T THAT GREAT. I HEARD HE WAS A **RUBBISH** BAKER.

WE CAN'T LET THIS HAPPEN! KING ALFRED IS MY GREAT GRANDFATHER - WELL, TIMES THIRTY.

THIS ISN'T YOUR HOME - DO YOU WANT TO COME WITH US AGAIN AND PUT THINGS RIGHT?

DEFINITELY!

MUM! WE MISSED YOU!

BUT I'VE ONLY BEEN IN THE SHOP FOR **FIVE** MINUTES!

WHERE DID JESSIE GET THAT COSTUME?

WE WERE TAKEN BY **TIME VIKINGS!** AND I JOINED THEIR CREW, BUT THEY THREW ME OUT.

AND THEN WE WENT TO THE FUTURE! AND THEN WE MET A BAKER CALLED ALFRED.

SHOPPING

THAT'S NICE DEAR.

GOODBYE, CAPTAIN CLOCK.

I HOPE I SEE YOU ALL AGAIN ONE DAY.